Ebelebe

Kyuka Lilymjok

ISBN 978-978-969-222-4

Published by:
Free Pen Publishers
10 Lachlan Close, Maitama, Abuja

Any people depicted in stock imagery provided by Thinkstock are models, and such images are being used for such purposes only.

This book is printed on acid-free paper.

The views expressed in this work are solely those of the author and do not necessarily reflect the views of the publisher. The publisher hereby disclaims any responsibility for them.

To my wife Maria and my children:
Justice, Sunfair and Fairprincess

No one eats war
It is war that eats people

Chapter One

First, it was a dove. For a while, it circled the sky over Petutu's house cooing in a melodious and soothing manner. This was rare among doves. Doves seldom coo in flight. They only cooed when perched on a tree or the ground. Soon the dove was joined by a hawk screeching disagreeably.

Standing in front of his house, Petutu watched the dove and the hawk circling the sky above while listening to coos and screeching. As the dove and the hawk circled the sky, the sky seemed to move along with the birds. As the dove cooed, the sky also seemed to coo with it. As the hawk screeched, the sky seemed to leak sorrow.

In ancient times before the coming of letters and the telephone, the dove and the hawk were the means of sending and receiving messages by Petutu's ancestors who could hear and speak to birds. While the chirchir bird was seen as the bearer of the bush telegraph, the dove and the hawk were seen as bearers of messages of great import from the ancestors.

One of the messages commonly sent and received from doves and hawks were messages of peace and war. Doves bore messages of peace while doves bore messages of war. Seeing the dove and hawk circling the sky cooing and screeching, Petutu wished he could understand birds' speech the way his ancestors did. 'Ebelebe!' he exclaimed. In Mandi language, Ebelebe means peace or war. He had just returned from a war death kept missing him by the skin of his teeth. The thought of another war so soon after the last one he was involved was a bee in his heart that stung badly.

Petutu had always liked doves. Few things excited him like waking up in the morning to the cooing of a dove. Strangely, he did not like pigeons which look like doves. The cooing of pigeons which he called clucking got on his nerves. Unlike doves, pigeons defecated everywhere. But perhaps more than any other reason, he resented pigeons because they had submitted themselves to domestication. Unlike doves that strive to survive in the jungle in freedom and dignity by their sweat, pigeons settle for the servile life of domestication so that they are fed by man. They were to him like dogs which he also despised. Any creature that could survive in dignity and freedom, but chose to be a tamed thing for food recommended itself for Petutu's contempt. Now watching the dove circling and cooing in the sky, he did not know whether it was the circling or cooing of the dove he loved more.

After sometime of circling alone, the dove and the hawk over Petutu's house were joined by other doves and hawks. Soon, the whole sky was overrun by doves and hawks. The doves and hawks in the sky were not a flock of doves and hawks, but a cloud of doves and hawks. As a cloud, they covered the sun. It seemed all the while the first dove and hawk were circling the sky cooing and screeching, they were calling other doves and hawks to join them. If this was the case, what were they calling them to join them in the sky for?

The sight he was beholding was surprising and shocking to Petutu. So, there were so many doves and hawks in the country as the multitude he was beholding? Then where have they been all the while? As they circled the sky, the doves kept cooing and the hawks screeching. The whole neighbourhood was now full of the cooing and screeching sounds of doves and hawks as its sky was clouded by them.

Whatever it was they were circling the sky and cooing for, it took the birds a while to accomplish. During this time, they not only own the sky over Baku village, they possessed the village. Not only Petutu was beholding them, other villagers were. Not only Petutu was surprised and shocked by their number, everyone in the village was. Only bats were known to command such numbers.

While Petutu was watching the flight of the doves and hawks listening to their cooing and screeching, he was joined by Oliki his neighbour. Oliki was one of those rare human beings that looked like a man and a woman mixed together. In body and voice, he was a man and a woman. His body was supple, yet steely. His voice was hoarse, yet soft. When with him, one moment the person with him would think he was with a man only to think he was with a woman the next moment. In addition to his hybridity, Oliki was a pessimistic man prone to depression. In one of his depressed moments, he had gone to Petutu's house one evening and told him he was going to the forest to commit suicide.

Petutu laughed. 'Oliki you are not serious,' he said still laughing. 'People who commit suicide don't go about telling the world they want to commit suicide. They sneak out of their houses to do so.'

Oliki left his house without saying anything and walked to the forest. After about an hour, he followed Oliki to the forest and found the latter warming himself by a fire he had kindled and was roasting yam in.

'Oliki, I told you this thing is not easy,' he said laughing.

Now Oliki was beside him looking at the birds circling the sky with him. 'What is the meaning of this?' he heard his neighbour asking.

'What is the meaning of what?' Petutu asked; his mind more in the sky than on the ground with Oliki.

'The meaning of what you are looking at and listening to,' Oliki said.

'If I know its meaning, I won't be gaping at it the way I am,' Petutu said still more in the sky than on the ground. By all appearance, he was flying, cooing and screeching in the sky with the birds.

'I have never seen anything like this before; have you?' Petutu heard Oliki asking.

'If I have, I wouldn't be this thrown by what I am seeing,' Petutu said joining Oliki on the ground. 'It's strange, beautiful and frightening.'

'This can't be for nothing,' Oliki said.

'I agree with you; this can't be for nothing,' Petutu said. 'But whatever, it is for I believe these birds mean well.'

'When the lizard nods its head, it does not always mean all is well,' Oliki said, despondently.

'True, but I think the lizards now nodding their heads in the sky are saying all is well,' Petutu said, sombrely.

'They are saying all is well for the sky or for us?' Oliki asked.

'I think they are saying all is well for both the sky and us,' Petutu said. 'Birds are children of the sky. They can't harbour evil for the sky.'

'They may not harbour evil for the sky; you may not be able to say the same thing about the earth,' Oliki said.

'Children of the sky are like the sky – benevolent beings,' Petutu said, trying to calm Oliki down. 'Only good comes from the sky. The sun comes from the sky; so does rain.'

'You are forgetting thunder and violent winds; these two also come from the sky,' Oliki said, tartly.

'How often does thunder and violent storms happen compared to how often the sun shines and rain falls?' Petutu asked, rhetorically.

'I even forgot, the hawk that pounces on chicks comes from the sky.'

'I can't see the sky weeping,' Petutu continued talking as if he had not heard what Oliki said. 'Speaking for myself, though I am not at ease over what I am seeing, my heart is telling me the birds in the sky are telling us evil is coming.'

'You are right there,' Oliki said. 'It is not only ear and mouth that hear and talk; the heart also hears and talk and the things the heart hears and talk are serious things that give life and take life. Premonition is the heart hearing things that are coming that can take life or give life.'

When the doves and hawks were done with flying, cooing and screeching, they filed out to distant climes watched in awe and enchantment by the village. While flying away, they were led by one of their numbers Petutu believed must be the dove and hawk that first circled the sky over his house.

Chapter Two

Petutu was an ex-service man. Either as a combatant or a soldier in peace-keeping operations, Petutu has seen action in different conflict zones around the world. He fought the Pokko war between his country and Tansar. The war was fought over Pokko Peninsula over which both nations asserted ownership. The Pokko war lasted three years during which millions of lives were lost.

He was a Sergeant during the war and fought as an infantry soldier. As a soldier, Petutu saw the gun as a barking sword. In shape, the gun looks like a sword. In function, the gun is a sword, only more devastating than the sword. While the sword has to strike at close range, the gun strikes from afar and with more deadly effect. While the sword strikes quietly, the gun strikes loudly to tell the world what it has done.

To Petutu, the barking sword – the gun, might not have been invented for war, its existence has placed the world on a warpath. Perhaps invented to bark at animals in the bush; the barking sword soon turned against man who invented it – a Frankenstein monster who sees man as the game he does not need to go to the bush to hunt.

During the Pokko war, the cooing of a dove woke him up in the morning in the jungle he and his fellow combatants slept. Fighting the previous day was intense. All day through, booming gun sounds raged through the jungle in wave after wave of attack of enemy positions. As guns boomed, death boomed. When the gun fell silent at dusk, Petutu and fellow combatants that survived the heavy fighting of that day fell back on their backs and slept off. When the cooing of the dove woke him in the morning of the following day, Petutu pinned his ears to the soulful tune of the dove's melody. Surrounded by the hostility and culpability of war, he was so moved by the peace and innocence that resonates through the dove's melody that he thought of deserting the war.

It turned out it was not only him that was woken up by the dove's cooing. Other soldiers were also woken up and like Petutu pinned their ears to it. Observing a fellow soldier who slept near him listening to the melody of the dove, Petutu said, 'What a great morning to be alive and listen to the cooing of this dove instead of the booming sounds of barking swords,' he said to the neighbouring soldier.

'Yeah, what a great morning,' the other soldier grunted. 'It is so refreshing and soothing. What is the dove saying?'

'How I wish I know.'

'Is it saying we should lay down our arms and flee the war?'

Petutu was shocked to hear what his fellow combatant said. So, he was not the only one thinking that way. 'I won't be surprised if that's what it is saying,' he said.

'Neither will I,' said the other soldier, 'I am getting tired and fed up with this bloody war that threatens beast as man.'

'I wish I can become a dove and fly away from this war,' Petutu said encouraged to speak his mind by what the other soldier was saying. 'It is all utterly pointless killing people who have not wronged me; people I don't even know.'

'If men cannot speak sense to themselves, it is good that birds should speak sense to them,' the other shoulder said also drawing courage from what Petutu was saying.

'I wish I am a dove that can speak sense to those fuelling this war,' Petutu said. 'I will tell them to take their fuel home and cook food with it.'

'The dove has never been able to speak sense to the hawk,' the other soldier said. 'The hawk is committed to violence. Belligerents are hawks.'

'While doves go to sleep, hawks are always awake around the world vomiting carnage here and there,' Petutu said.

'That is the problem,' the other soldier said. 'While angels go to sleep, the devil and his demons never go to sleep.'

'It is sad,' Petutu said, a sorrowful look overtaking his face. He was recalling the death toll of the war and destruction of property by it. The previous day he and Ekete – a fellow combatant were behind an encampment shooting when Ekete was hit by a grenade thrown at their barricade by the Tansar forces. Ekete's head was turned into a mass of blood some of which splashed on him. Amazingly, he was unscathed by the grenade. Though Ekete was dying, there was no time for him to touch him, if not to help him, to express sympathy over his condition. He had to keep firing to ward off attack on him. It was only after doing so that he turned to the dying man.

Before the attack that killed Ekete, he had narrowly escaped death by a roadside bomb planted by the Tansar forces. They were travelling in an open van when the bomb had detonated throwing the van upside down. He was the only one that survived that attack. Because of his several narrow escapes from death in the course of the war, he had come to accept as true the saying that each bullet has its billet. However, that he held this belief had neither stopped him from agonizing over the war nor even minimized in a significant manner his fear in the war.

A week after Petutu and fellow combatants were woken up by the cooing of the dove in the warfront, the Pokko war ended. The answer to *Ebelebe* was peace, not war. Another week after the war ended, Petutu retired from the army.

Chapter Three

In the jungle of Etete, there was a quiet flowing stream that flowed in the dry as the rainy season. This stream, called Ahok stream, was also popularly called the stream of the dead. It was called the stream of the dead because it was believed the dead fetched their drinking water from it. Many people who had gone to the stream said they saw ghostly beings bending to fetch water from the stream. Others said they heard voices without seeing those talking, while others said they heard footsteps of people or people coughing without seeing those walking or coughing. There was a shimmering quality about the stream that was bound to wake in anyone feelings of both reverence and awe.

While still serving in the military, whenever Petutu was in Fakwa his village, he visited Ahok stream. When he retired from service and returned home, no week passed without him going to the stream. He said he went to the stream to commune with nature and his ancestors. Each time he visited the stream, he had a feeling of being in ethereal territory. The water of the stream, the trees that flanked it and the reeds twirling round the trees were all very charming and sobering.

Petutu was not the usual man who went to usual places. He was the unusual man who went to unusual places. Ahok stream was an unusual place. Petutu went to it frequently. Sitting by the bank of the stream, he said he saw shadowy, ashy human figures walking the banks of the stream and bending over the stream to fetch water. He said he also heard whispers and murmurs in the air about him.

Sitting by the stream seeing the images he said he saw and hearing whispers and murmurs he said he heard, he occasionally asked who is speaking over there and who is bending over there. But often, he sat quietly by the stream in supplication to nature and his ancestors.

Petutu attributed his narrow escapes from death in the battle field to nature and his ancestors. His fraternity with nature and his ancestors he saw as the talisman that secured him from death. Like the devil, the dead take care of their own.

When he returned from the Pokko war, Petutu went to Ahok stream to commune with nature and his ancestors. While at the battle front, he longed for the stream. It was therefore not surprising that as soon as he returned home from the war and military service, he went to the stream. Sitting by the stream, he could see shadowy and ashy human images bending over the stream to fetch water. He could hear whispers and murmurs in the air about him. He was excited by what, if true, would have scared silly the usual man.

While sitting by the stream, a whiff of dry grass floated by followed by a broken piece of calabash Petutu wondered where it was coming from. Ahok stream started in the forest and ended in the forest. Where then was the broken calabash coming from? Could it be a broken calabash from the dead? He stood up and entered the stream to recover it from the stream and look at it.

It was the usual piece of a broken calabash. He threw it back into the stream and it continued its journey downstream. He resumed his former seat. Behind him a bird chirped. He looked back but could not see the bird. Above him the sky was rumbling. The sky was cooking rain. Very soon what it was cooking would be served on earth.

Sitting by the stream, his mind went back to the war and a burden he carried in his heart. Before his death in the battle field, Ekete his fallen comrade had given him messages to take to his wife. He only met Ekete two days to the latter's death when they found themselves fighting alongside each other. They quickly took to each other and began talking as if they were old friends.

Most of what they talked about was the war and whether they were going to survive it. So Petutu knew little about Ekete and the latter's family until he was hit by the grenade and wanted Petutu to take messages to his wife. Ekete could only tell him he lived in Tarako province, but could not tell him which district of the big province he lived before he closed his mouth in death.

In the throes of death, Ekete with hands clasping at his military uniform had grunted to him that he should tell his wife how much he loved her and that in his next reincarnation, he would like to still be her husband. He should also tell her he owed Honga fifty thousand dilas and Jele owed him a hundred thousand dilas. His wife knew both men. She should collect his money from Jele and pay Honga. The balance, she should put to her beneficial use. He then groped into his pocket and fished out a leather bangle he said his wife should give to their son. He opened his mouth again, but could not say anything. He was dead. Now Petutu was saddled with tracing his wife and delivering his messages.

Chapter Four

Tienko country was a very big country. Tarako province where Ekete's wife lived was a big province. Not knowing which district Ekete's wife lived in this huge district left Petutu bewildered on how to go look for her to deliver her husband's messages. Not knowing anyone who knew Ekete from who he would get some information on the fallen man, he was left with only the legion office as the place he could go to find some information that might lead him to the deceased's wife.

A few days after arriving home from the war, Petutu set out to look for Ekete's wife. It was a dull, unexciting day Petutu feared might rub off his mission. The previous night, he had discussed his trip with his wife. Initially, she had sought to discourage him considering the time and expenses involved and the lack of benefit of the trip to him and his family.

'You said you only met at the warfront?' his wife asked him.

'Yes, we only met at the warfront,' he said. 'We actually met only a day to his death.'

'I don't think you should waste your time and suffer yourself on a wild goose chase like this,' his wife said.

Petutu knew his wife very well. Though she had not mentioned money, he knew she was more concerned about the money he would spend going to look for Ekete's wife than him suffering himself. From root to branch, she was a mercenary in her perception and patronage of life. Wherever a nickel was to be made, she was there. Wherever a nickel was to be lost, she was not there. 'My dear, geese are there to be chased now and then,' he said to her in a jovial tone. 'Though a goose chase seldom brings in either eggs or meat, but on luck, it sometimes brings in eggs or meat. I don't enjoy goose chasing; but what can I do? Having assured a dying man I will deliver his messages to his wife, I am bound in honour to do so.'

'I understand your situation and sentiments,' his wife said. 'But the money; think of the money you are going to spend trying to trace his wife. Money, you know we don't have and need badly.'

It was now out what he knew must come out. Nickels were about to be lost and his wife was pulling him away from where they would be lost. 'I know we need the money I will spend tracing

Ekete's wife, but my conscience is not giving me a choice in the matter,' he said.

'It is better conscience is sick than the purse is sick,' his wife murmured, dryly.

'My dear wife, I am committed to delivering Petutu's messages,' he said in a firm voice.

'I am not with you in that commitment,' his wife said with languor in her voice. 'I am even beginning to wonder if beside the messages, there is something else you want to deliver to her.'

'What was that?' he asked in a sharp tone.

'That was that,' she retorted. 'I am wondering if outside digging out his wife to deliver his messages, someone wants to dig into other things. I am also wondering if there are even messages to be delivered.'

'Watch your tongue woman,' he said in a heated voice. Though his wife could be audacious, she often retreated when the danger signal was up and bleeping. The note of anger in his voice was a danger signal that told her to retreat and she did. Danger signal apart, she knew her husband was not a philandering man and so she had nothing to fear about him looking for Ekete's wife. She made her insinuations only out of spite, not out of suspicion of her husband cheating on her.

Out of his house on his trip to Tarako, Petutu went to the motor park to board a vehicle. On his way to the motor park, his mind was on the mild altercation between him and his wife the previous night over his trip. 'What a woman!' he exclaimed; 'very intelligent and impudent, yet very obedient and submissive.' Despite their disagreement in the night over the trip, she was all cheer in the morning as she bade him farewell when he was leaving the house for the trip.

At the motor park, Petutu met an *agbero* – a motor park tout, he knew in the motor park more than twenty years ago. 'You are still here?' he asked the *agbero*.

'Have you ever seen or heard of an *agbero* that became something else or left the motor park?' the *agbero* asked him in return. 'I am still here. In fact, I am now the prince of the motor park.'

Petutu laughed as he pressed further into the motor park.

On his way to the motor park, Petutu had thought of the bad road he would travel to Tarako on. Long ago, a man sang this song for the roads of Tienko:

I wanted the road to carry me
somewhere
So I went to the road but found
The road was not at home.
I was told by the river
Flowing where the road used to be
That the road has travelled.
River, when the road returns,
Please tell it to come and see me,
For I too want to travel.

Further into the motor park, Petutu found there were many buses and cabs all looking for passengers to Tarako. In Tienko, both roads and vehicles were scraps. So, in the motor park, Petutu found that neither buses nor cabs looked roadworthy. As the vehicles were not roadworthy, the roads they plied were also not motorable. When therefore a vehicle hit the road, there was bound to be a quarrel between it and the road. The vehicle would be saying, you are not worthy of me, and the road would be saying you also are not worthy of me. The vehicle would be saying go to hell, and the road would also be saying go to hell. In the end sometimes, the vehicle, the passengers in it and the road all went to hell. This happened when there was an accident passengers were maimed or killed, the vehicle was wrecked or the road was scorched by an accident vehicle that has ignited.

Though there was often not much to choose between buses and cabs as far as comfort and speed were concerned, cabs often charged higher fares more out of a sentimental value than any utility value. Petutu knew this. Wanting to make some savings, he boarded a bus since paying a higher fare in a cab would neither secure him more comfort nor get him to Tarako faster.

Chapter Five

In Pokko Peninsula the carnage left behind by the war was hissing and smouldering like a mountain ape. Inside the city, buildings had been reduced to rubbles. Mangled and twisted iron rods lie among pulverised blocks and dust wherever one turned in the bombed city. The bombed buildings were the carcasses the iron rods were the bones of. While some buildings had been completely levelled down by bombs, some had been reduced to gaping caves.

At the edge of the Peninsula near the sea, a building hit by a bomb had one part of it on the ground while the other part was standing. The part standing looked like a giant cave in Slovenia. Wind from the nearby sea blew into it generating eerie sounds one might associate with lamentations of ancient spirits. A lonely passer-by hearing the sound of the wind thought so. He stood by forlornly without a sense of either waiting for someone or resting before moving on. If sounds coming from the collapsed building were lamentations of spirits, were the lamentations of the spirits of people that were killed during the war or some other spirits? The passer-by further wondered.

Sometimes the wind whined and whistled inside the partly destroyed building like a widow mourning her dead husband or a hunter whistling to his dogs. Was the widow whining over the grave of her husband? There was no human grave where she was. The only grave there was, was the grave of human misadventure. Was the hunter whistling to the dogs of war? There was nothing for the dogs of war to fasten their fangs into except the mangled and twisted iron rods, dust and ashes of ruin.

Sometimes the wind inside the cavy building instead of whistling or whining, gurgled as if some animals inside it were fighting. At some point, it gurgled in such a fierce manner that made the passer-by wonder if animals were actually fighting inside the collapsed building but he could not see them. Twice he passed the palm of his hand over his eyes and refocused his vision but saw nothing.

The wind from the sea seemed to intensify. The eerie sounds from the cavy building seemed to intensify too. The passer-by still stood by listening to the wind. Though motionless and inert in limbs, he was very active in mind. Was the wind lamenting over the war? Was it grieving over the many lives and property that were destroyed by the war or was it angry with the folly of the war? Was the sea angry with the way the partly collapsed building was gaping at it or it was sorrowing over its own loss in the war? Were Davy Jones from the sea in the wind from the sea and they were the ones making the esoteric fearful noises? Beside the solitary passer-by, no one was about the ruins of the building to sense the sorrow oozing out of it.

From the passive and disinterested way the passer-by was looking at the ruins about him, it could easily be inferred he had no intimate relationship with the ruined buildings or even the city, but was merely one who happened by a scene of destruction and desolation. A dull, disinterested look in his eyes communicated his lack of intimacy with the ruins about him like nothing would have.

Outside the city, the sky over the Peninsula looked molten in some places and overcast in other places while the sun seemed not too well either. Where the sky looked molten, the solitary passer-by wondered whether the war had melted the sky there. Where it looked overcast, he wondered if the war was causing it to weep there.

By a tree in the midst of the ruins, two crows hopped about in gaiety that contrasted sharply with the desolation about them. What were they hopping about over? The passer-by could not say. Was there a party somewhere only they were privy to? How did they even survive the war and were about? Why did they not flee the war zone like other birds and animals? He had wandered by the fringes of the destruction wrought by the war, he had not seen any animal or human being until he came by the crows which were not only hale, but seemed quite hearty.

Chapter Six

The Pokko war not only maimed the city, it maimed the jungle. It not only maimed man, it maimed trees and beasts. That was perhaps why birds in the jungle took to the skies over human habitations. They were most likely lamenting the war and celebrating its end.

Blistering chemical weapons like mustard and phosgene used in the war killed many trees. Because trees were used as shields by combatants, they took bullets and grenades meant for men. Because they could not run or duck, they were hit by all types of mortars. A huge tree in Feemel forest known as *hunk of the forest* was frequently used as shield by combatants. Because it was frequently used as a shield, it was battered by bullets and grenades. What was left of it was finished off by chemical weapons. It died even before the war ended.

Animals that could run did not significantly fare better. Choking chemical weapons like chlorine and phosgene used in the war killed many animals. Landmines lay in some parts of the forest blew off the limbs of many animals that stepped on them. Sometime running only delivered animals to worst harm. A deer amputated by a landmine it stepped on while running from the war limped across a highway squealing and howling. It was no doubt in great pains. Fortunately, it was missed by a lorry rattling down the road. Squealing and howling as it ran faster to avoid being hit by the lorry was heart-wrenching. A chimpanzee shot on the hip by a combatant of the belligerent forces dragging itself across a highway was not as lucky as the deer. It was crushed by a fast-moving tanker. A monkey wounded in the head by a bullet was wandering a highway dazed by its trauma but was lucky to be rescued by a man in a truck. The man was a forest guard with a passion for animal preservation. He took the monkey into his truck and drove it to the forestry he was guard.

In the forest, the forest guard proceeded to talk to the monkey as if it was a human being. 'From every indication you have been maimed by this senseless war,' he began, cuddling the monkey. 'Hear me talk of senseless war as if any war is sensible. All wars are not only senseless, they are stupid. I believe you and other animals in the jungle must be totally bewildered by this carnage called war.'

For a while the forest guard said nothing; then began talking again. 'You are not only wounded, I believe you are hungry. Where will you find food in a forest of booming guns, burning grass, blistering and choking agents? Even when you find the food, where will you find the peace to eat it? It is all very unfortunate.' Again, he lapsed into silence. 'Not to worry,' he said at last. 'I will take good care of you until you are fit again.'

In Pinke, a wounded elephant wandered into the town looking thoroughly distressed and disoriented. It was a frightening sight to many especially those who had not seen an elephant before. Limping and snorting, once the elephant trumpeted and many people scampered in fear. For a long while, the elephant wandered through the city in pain while people stared at it in shock and awe. Many were afraid of the elephant though it was wounded. It was an hour after it wandered into the town that it was shot down by a man who saw it when it first entered the town and went back home to load his gun. After loading his gun, he trailed the elephant to where he shot it down. Everyone was startled by the booming sound of the gun and shocked seeing the elephant going down in a hideous heap.

For a while the people stood speechless looking at the man and the elephant he had shot. It was like people were under a spell which only wore off when the elephant which had been kicking in the throes of death lay still in death. It was then someone in the crowd yelled in jubilation of what the man did only to be rebuked by another person not happy with what the man did.

Because of the war, animals in their habitats in the forest suddenly found themselves thrown out of the forest to towns, villages, cities and highways where in most cases they met their death. With choking agents, gun sounds ricocheting through the forest and smoke billowing out of it, many animals found the forest a house of death. As a victim of the war, the forest was no less whimpering and wailing than human victims of the war; neither was it having less nightmares over the war.

As animals were forced out of the forest by the war, so were several forest human communities forced out of it. Forest communities that for ages had lived in the forest where they derived their livelihood found themselves caught in the crossfire of belligerent forces and had to flee for dear lives. After the war, two men from a forest community on returning to the forest were shocked and angry over what the war did to the forest. Though they were shocked and angry over what the war did to the forest generally, they were more shocked and angry over what it did to *hunk of the forest*.

'This is very bad,' one of the men said. 'They killed *hunk of the forest*.'

'It is indeed very bad killing a tree that had nothing to do with the war,' said the other man. 'Man is both a pernicious and an annoying tick.'

'*Hunk of the forest*, home to the forest as the forest was home to it is no more,' said the first man. '*Hunk of the forest* was the soul of the forest. Not much of the forest is left without it.'

The forest was the theatre the war was fought with guns, landmines, grenades, chemical weapons and death acting before a horrified and pained audience. It was the theatre war operations always ending in the mortuary were carried out. Long after the war, the forest was sick not only from physical wounds inflicted on it, but from the trauma of the war. No effort was ever made to heal the sick forest by those that made it sick.

Chapter Seven

Petutu's trip to Tarako was a bumpy and eventful trip. The rickety bus he boarded was swaying from side to side while barking forward like a famished and angry dog. And there was no doubt it was hungry for an overhaul and angry that this food had not come its way for a long time. While swaying from side to side and barking forward, the boneshaker was hurling insult at the dilapidated road for worsening its condition. All the way the vehicle was crawling forward, it kept searching where there was still meat on the road it could sink its teeth into with less pain, but rarely found such meat – hence it kept barking angrily. The road was more loudly a drag in a literal than a colloquial sense.

While listening to the bus barking at the road, it suddenly dawned on Petutu that a dog only growls and barks when gnawing at a bone and it growls and barks out of anger of a bone being thrown to it instead of meat. When meat is thrown to a dog, the dog does not growl or bark when eating the meat. This realization dawning on him, when the rickety vehicle growled and barked at the bad road, he not only understood its feelings, he felt for it. It was a dog growling and barking at bones thrown to it. Whenever the road got better, it then had meat and did not growl or bark.

As the vehicle was barking at the road, the road full of potholes and ditches wasn't excited by the old bucket either. The old bus by its squeals and sways was getting on its nerves. As the bus crawled forward on the road, passengers in the boneshaker swayed to and fro like dancers in a samba dance or rockers in a rock dance. When the vehicle entered a pothole or ditch more violently, oaths and curses of the road and the government followed in swift paces and generous tons so much that it seemed oaths and curses by the passengers were much swifter and generous than the road and the bus.

When the bus squealed, the squeal sounded to Petutu like the mewing of a cat on the trail of a rat. The bus and the people inside it were the cat while the road and the government that owned it but failed to repair it were the rat. Petutu found the analogy very apt. The bus like most cats was milky and the road like most rats was black. The bus was carrying hungry and angry people that could devour the government they see as a thieving rat – a thieving rat that neglected the road.

The rat was fleeing the cat in a funny way. It was fleeing backward into the mouth of the cat. Here and there, previous cats that had chased the rat Petutu's cat was now chasing had bitten the rat leaving pock-marks – potholes, on the rat.

Petutu was sitting near a younger man who more than anyone in the bus was cursing the government for the derelict state of the road. Not only was he cursing and swearing at the government more than anyone, he seemed to be sweating and swaying more than anyone. One would have thought that given his age, he would be firmer in body and sway less. Alas, this was not the case. It was older persons with weaken bodies that were swaying less. Not only was the young man cursing and swearing at the government, he was swearing and cursing older generations saying they were responsible for the rundown state of the nation which the road was part of.

'You are right holding older generations responsible for the deplorable condition of the road, but do you think your own generation will necessarily do better?' Petutu asked him, irritation gnawing at his heart.

'My generation will surely do better,' the young man answered rapidly.

'How?'

'Because we are young and energetic.'

What an answer! Petutu thought. The young man's answer reminded him of a man he once described as clean outside but dirty inside; walking well with his legs but limping in the head; well-formed outside but ill-formed inside. 'Just because you are young and energetic, you will do better?' he probed the youth for better intelligence.

'Yes, just because we are young and strong,' the young man said.

'Is governance about youth and strength or about patriotism, ideas, and courage to give effect to ideas?' Petutu asked the young man further.

'It is about running and you guys are crawling. It is about action and we the youth have the strength for action,' the young man said.

'Before action, there is a process called thinking; what value do you allocate to thinking in governance?' Petutu asked.

'Yes, thinking is there; but action is needed to give value to thinking,' the young man said. 'Strength is needed for action.'

You are right,' Petutu said. 'But even this strength you keep harping on that the youth have, here in this bus, you who is younger than everyone has been swaying more than everyone. Does your swaying suggest strength or weakness?'

'I thought I was the only one seeing how he has been swaying like a reed in the wind,' a man sitting directly behind the young man said. 'I thought part of the reason this vehicle is swaying is its old age; that a newer vehicle would have swayed less. But seeing a young man swaying more than we the old ones is beginning to make me think otherwise.'

'The youths of this age are a wonderful bunch,' a passenger sitting beside the one that just spoke said. 'While the old might be said to have mucus in their brains that need clearing, the youth keep exhibiting signs of having bones in their heads that need dissolution into brains.'

At this point the vehicle had almost come to a full stop. It had almost completely been swallowed by a ditch it had crawled into and was climbing out of. Ahead of the ditch were a group of policemen at a checkpoint checking vehicles for what they did not even know.

In Tienko the standard practice of policemen was to set up checkpoints either on portions of the road that were exceptionally bad or at bends. This was to ensure stubborn or devious drivers did not drive past them without stopping. When they position themselves where the road was full of potholes or bumps, as the so-called sleeping policemen would be flagging the driver to stop, the awake policemen would also be flagging him to stop.

Police's insistence that vehicles, particularly commercial vehicles, stop at their checkpoints is not so much about checking the vehicles for faults as about squeezing money out of the drivers of the vehicles. When they stopped vehicles where there were potholes, the potholes turned to begging bowls drivers dropped crumbled Petan notes. Out of contempt, most drivers instead of giving petan notes to police hand to hand, dropped the notes in potholes and sped on.

As the vehicle Petutu was travelling in climbed out of the ditch, it was flagged down by the police who had their guns in shooting position as if the vehicle was a game and they were hunters. The driver of the vehicle who either was an ex-policeman or had worked with the police flashed an identity card at them saying, 'esprit de corps.'

'The policemen at the checkpoint waved him on while positioning themselves against vehicles behind the one they had waved on.

'Esprit de corps has become the password for corruption in this country,' someone in front of Petutu lamented.

'That's very true,' another passenger said. 'Every corrupt person is looking out for his kind. Corrupt judges moved by esprit de corps free corrupt judges standing trial in their courts. It is sad.'

'Corrupt judges swayed by esprit de corps not only free judges standing trial for corruption in their courts, they free anyone standing trial for corruption in their courts.'

'A vicious clan of corrupt people had since evolved in this country,' another passenger said. This passenger had hardly stopped talking when the vehicle they were travelling in swerved to avoid a pothole only to fall into a ditch. It fell on its side. Passengers screaming and shrieking scrambled to get out of the vehicle.

Chapter Eight

At Ekete's house in the small town of Ase in Tarako province, his wife was mourning the death of her husband while his children were mourning the death of their father. It was only the previous day they received news of his death at the warfront.

The widow of the fallen man was sitting on the bare dusty floor of the courtyard in her widow's weeds. She kept throwing her legs and hands about while crying inconsolably. Sometimes her hands tore at the loose hair on her head; sometimes she scooped dust from the ground and let it roll through her fingers. As she wailed, mucus was coming from her nose as tears were from her eyes.

About three women were seated around the mourning widow all trying to calm her down. But all their efforts seemed to lag behind the delirious pace of her grief. Looking vacantly ahead of her and about her, she seemed out of her mind and even out of her body. Twice, she had stood up against the restraining hands of the women and dashed towards the entrance of the house. Each time the three women had ran after her to bring her back.

As she cried, she kept saying, 'So I am now a widow! Delu, it is not fair. 'You are gone leaving me with the children, who will help me take care of them? Death, you are not fair.'

Near the entrance of the house, two old men sitting on a long plank of wood placed on two stones were talking and shaking their heads in grief. 'It is not death that is not fair; it is war that is not fair,' said one of the old men to the other. What he said was in apparent response to what the mourning widow was saying.

'You are right,' said the other old man. 'It is war that is not fair. Death was sitting in the bush minding its business, but war would not let it be. If war had not created the occasion, death wouldn't have created the tears. If the chick does not stray into the bush, the hawk would not pounce on it. '

'If not for war, how can a young man like Ekete die leaving old men like us to bury him?' said the first old man.

'Why should a person die for a quarrel between two people?' the second old man asked rhetorically. 'If our government is quarrelling with Tansar government over Pokko, why should our son die over their quarrel? He did not ask them to quarrel. If Pokko is seized from Tansar, it would not be brought to his father's house.'

Honga and Jele were among the mourning crowd in Ekete's compound. While Honga was mourning, Jele was only putting up a show of doing so. Honga was mourning because he lent money to Ekete that the dead man was yet to repay. With his death, recovering his money was going to become tricky if not impossible. Ekete's wife was not likely to know about the money her husband owed him. Even if she knew, he would feel somehow and it would look somehow going to ask a poor widow to repay money he was being owed by her dead husband. Not only Ekete died, his money died with him. His worst fears had come to pass. When he heard that Ekete had been mobilized to the warfront, his heart had sunk. Will his money return from the war? he kept wondering fearfully to himself. Now sitting in Ekete's compound, the grim reality of his situation hit him. 'My money,' he blurted out involuntarily carried away by his thoughts and grief.

'What was that?' Jele asked.

'Nothing,' Honga said, trying to recover himself from his thoughts and be part of what was going on in Ekete's house if only for the sake of appearances.

'I thought I heard you mentioning money,' Jele said making and unmaking his face, his eyes darting snakingly here and there.

'I guess I was carried away by my thoughts,' Honga said, standing up to stretch himself.

Unlike Honga,' Jele was full of happiness. While putting up an appearance of grief, inside him he was glowing with happiness. Ekete's money was with him. Now Ekete was dead. It was not likely that the dead man's wife knew about the money. This means the money was now his. The war over Pokko was good. If other people suffer losses in the war, he gained. He had spent some of Ekete's money with him to marry a new wife. So he did not need to go looking for money to repay Ekete. What remained of the money, he would put into some business that would help him maintain his wives. 'Great!' he involuntarily muttered.

'What was that?' Honga asked, puzzled by what Jele said and the expression on his face.

'Sorry, I was lost in my thoughts,' Jele said trying to compose his face into a mourning mood.

'You said great! 'What is great about death?' Honga asked the puzzle on his face turning into a scowl.

'Like I said, I was carried away by my thoughts; can't someone think again?' Jele said now looking very much like everyone in the compound of the bereaved – a man in mourning.

Chapter Nine

Where the bus Petutu was travelling in fell was a forest. There was no town or village near the place. On both sides of the road, the forest surrounding the place stretched to the end of one's vision. Usually, a farm or some type of trees marked or suggest the presence of villages or towns nearby. There was no farm in sight and also no tree pointing to a village.

The passengers in the bus after evacuating the vehicle were able to get it back on its feet by pushing and tugging at it. But when the driver tried starting it, it only gave a squealing sound, but did not start. The bus was severely damaged by the fall. The vehicle would not move further from that point until it was repaired by a mechanic.

A bus Petutu initially wanted to board drove past the broken-down vehicle and its passengers. When the bus was driving past, its conductor who seemed to recognize Petutu mocked him with his eyes and the jeering smile on his face.

Petutu looked away feeling bad. His hand went into his pocket for his handset but the phone was not there. He went into the bus to look for it, but it was not in the bus either. He looked for it in the grass about the bus, but did not find it. He fell into further despair. He wanted to call his wife to tell her the mishap on the road. He was not good in memorising telephone numbers; so he did not know her number by heart.

Distress was palpable on the faces of the stranded passengers. Given where the bus was, it would take a long time for it to be fixed. During that time, what would they be eating or where would they even be sleeping? They might be lucky to find other vehicles to board and continue their journey; but would their driver be ready to give them part of their transport fares to do so?

A passenger walked to the driver and asked that he be given part of his transport fare for him to board another vehicle.

'I have no money to give you,' the driver snapped.

'But I paid you money; everyone here paid you,' the passenger said waving his hand in a curve to express himself by action as by words.

'And I paid your money to the petrol station,' the driver said, petulantly. 'You all saw me giving your money to the petrol attendant.'

'You people drive rickety vehicles that are not maintained only to leave passengers stranded on the road in the middle of nowhere; it is not fair,' the passenger lamented, lamely.

'Instead of delivering us to Tarako, you delivered us to a ditch,' said a second passenger joining the other passenger and the driver on the road.

'You were doing *esprit the corps* with the police, why couldn't you do the same with the potholes and ditches?' said a third passenger.

'It is sad. You don't maintain your vehicles and it is your passengers that always pay for your negligence,' said the first passenger that accosted the driver for his money.

'With what are we to maintain the vehicles?' the driver retorted; 'with the miserable fares passengers like you pay? By the way, it wasn't my vehicle that failed us; it was the road. If anyone should pay you, it should be the road or the government that neglects the road. Ask the road or the government to pay you.'

Petutu was incensed by the uncouth attitude of the driver, but kept his cool. At the right time, he would walk to the irritant and demand refund of his money. If the driver refuses to refund it, he would be shocked what he would do to him.

'This driver get liver o,' said a passenger who had been sitting alone listening to the altercation between the driver and other passengers. This passenger looked like a dark cloud that had detached itself from the sky and now walked the earth threatening to fall on anyone that annoyed him. He was rude in atmosphere as he was at heart. Now up on his feet and walking to where the driver and other passengers were, he looked like a retired thug weary of his retirement. The rude attitude of the driver to their plight looked like it was recalling him from his retirement. 'You de craze,' he said crowding in on the driver. '*Wetin* you *de* yearn so, dog shit?'

The driver who was all steel before was now melting like wax. ' You go fork out the money or I fuck you out?' the thug-passenger said bearing down on the driver, violence in him seething and itching for release.

Petutu looking at the driver smiled to himself. He may not need to do anything after all. The thug-passenger looking like he was just coming out of a conference with the devil was already doing what he would have done.

As the driver's hand was going to his pocket for the money the thug-passenger demanded, a bus carrying five men came to a storming halt where the broken vehicle was with its passengers.

'Hold it!' one of the men in the bus that just arrived shouted, jumping down with a gun in firing position. He was soon followed by other three men with him all carrying guns in firing positions. The driver was on the driving seat with the engine of the vehicle running.

The five men were kidnappers. Their camp was not too far from where the bus Petutu was travelling in fell and refused to start. Passengers in the bus thinking they were in the middle of nowhere suddenly found themselves in the middle of kidnappers.

'Oyah, get into our bus,' the leader of the kidnapping gang ordered passengers of the broken-down vehicle.

Petutu was incensed. He won't take orders from a thug while he remained a military man. He would look for an opening and strike. But how would he be able to handle four hoodlums all armed with guns? Well, he was not alone. If he starts something other passengers, particularly the thug-passenger, would most likely move in to help seeing they were in the same mess.

Passengers in the broken-down vehicle began filing into the bus as they were commanded. When Petutu moved close to the kidnapper standing by the door of the bus, his fist flashed at the kidnapper. The kidnapper, not expecting the punch, could not avoid it. Petutu's fist almost tore off his head from his neck. He felt backward his gun falling on top of him.

The other kidnappers were all taken by surprise by this attack. In all their operations, they had never encountered a hostage with this audacity. Though they held their guns in firing positions they never thought they would actually have to fire them because of resistance from hostages.

Other passengers seeing the delayed response by the kidnappers instead of coming to the aid of Petutu stood gaping at him and the kidnappers who soon recovered from their shock and came swinging at Petutu. Petutu aimed another punch at the leader of the kidnapping gang, but the latter shifted his head to one side and Petutu's fist hit space. The leader of the kidnappers landed two solid punches on Petutu's chest and stomach while the fist of a snarling kidnapper crashed into his back. He led out a painful groan and stretched out on the ground.

'You will pay dearly for this,' he heard the leader of the kidnapping gang swearing at him. 'After collecting the ransom on your head, I will kill you in the most painful way that in your next life you will not mess with guys like us.'

The kidnappers tied Petutu's hands behind him, hoisted him up and threw him into the bus. Other passengers were kicked into the bus and it stormed out of the road into the forest where the kidnappers' hideout was.

Inside the bus, the kidnappers stationed themselves at the back, middle and in front of the vehicle, their guns pointing menacingly at their captives. The kidnapper behind the vehicle looked like the first son of a monster. With bloodshot eyes, a vicious snarl that could recommend him for a sentry job in hell, he looked like a man outside the cult of human kindness and loose from the bonds of human pity. He did not need much encouragement to shoot anyone.

Chapter Ten

At the kidnappers' hideout the leader of the kidnappers looking fierce and savage informed all the passengers they had all been kidnapped and should begin thinking of those who would pay the ransom that would be placed on their heads. After this, he commanded the hostages to bring out all the money in their pockets and drop it on the ground. They all did so quickly except Petutu who looked at them with disgust while they were all frantic to empty their pockets.

'Your money!' the leader of the kidnappers barked at Petutu.

'The one you gave me or the one I borrowed from you?' Petutu hissed.

The leader of the kidnappers looking like a demon the devil left behind when going to hell, walked to Petutu, howled him up, slapped him and frisked his pockets for money. He found the money he was looking for in Petutu's front pockets and brought it out. With his hands tied behind, there was little Petutu could do.

'Great,' the leader of the kidnappers mused after he and his men had counted the money they had robbed their captives of. 'With this money, we will feed you until your relations or the government can bail you by the ransoms we will demand.'

The kidnappers' hideout inside the forest was a big shack under a tree surrounded by rocks. Inside the shack, sturdy pegs captives were tired to were half buried in the ground. Passed through the pegs were white chains captives were tied to.

The wall of the shack was constructed with bamboo and raffia sticks while the roof was made up of shrub leaves and raffia leaves. The ground was bare and looked like it had been trampled upon a lot lately.

Petutu and his fellow passengers were taken into the shack where they found two other captives – a boy and a girl. Immediately they were taken in, they were forced to sit down and chained to the pegs.

For a while the leader of the kidnappers stood looking at his hostages not saying anything. It seemed he was trying to make up his mind about something. When he made up his mind, he ordered the hostages to bring out their handsets. All hostages did as they were commanded, except Petutu who had lost his handset and whose hands were tied behind him.

'Where is your handset?' the leader of the kidnappers barked at him, slapping him at the same time.

Petutu spat on him.

The leader of the kidnappers went on punching him until he passed out. He then went through his pockets, but found no handset. 'No problem, you will produce it when you come to,' he swore under his breath. 'If you swallowed it, you will vomit it when I handle you next time.'

From Petutu, the leader of the kidnappers walked to his hostage that looked like he was from favourable financial circumstances. His looks apart, he was the passenger who brought out more money from his pocket when the hostages were commanded to do so. This leaned support to the thinking of the kidnappers' kingpin that he was well heeled.

'Use your handset and call the person you think will pay the ransom we will demand on your head,' the leader of the kidnappers commanded him.

With his hands shaking visibly, the hostage dialled his wife's number. When the phone began ringing, the kidnapper stretched his hand and collected it.

Soon the wife's voice sounded through the phone. 'Hello my darling,' she cooed into the phone.

'Well, it is not your darling,' the kidnapper barked into the phone. 'It is your damned you.'

For a while the wife did not say anything. If the kidnapper meant to rattle her the way he spoke, it seemed he succeeded. Her husband could almost hear her breathing on the other side. 'Who are you?' she asked when she could pull herself together.

'Good girl,' the kidnapper said in a voice that sounded more human than the grating one he used earlier. 'Who I am is not important. What is important is that I have your husband with me and will only release him to you if you pay ten million dilas to me within the next three days. If you fail to pay the money, pieces of your husband's body would be delivered to you in such gruesome parts that you would curse the day you married him.'

The hostage listening to the kidnapper caught his breath hearing what the kidnapper was saying to his wife. He was all bathed in sweat. This is utter madness. Ten million dilas! Where would his wife find that kind of money to bail him? His wife on the other side of the line was also sweating and breathing heavily. This time, he could hear her breathing.

Other hostages hearing what the kidnapper had told the wife of their fellow captive were petrified. Their fate would not be different from that of the hostage whose wife the kidnapper had just spoken to. Petutu who had come to was however not worked-up like the other hostages. It was not that he did not believe the kidnappers would carry out their threat if they were not paid; it was that he was indifferent to what they would do to him or other hostages. Several times, he had been in death situations, but had survived. If this claims his life, so be it.

'Ten million dilas?' the hostage's wife mourned into the phone. 'Where would I find that kind of money?'

'That is your headache,' the kidnappers' czar said. 'Ten million dilas in three days or your husband comes under the knife,' he barked into the phone, then cut the connection.

All hostages in the shack exchanged fearful glances. The chilly atmosphere in the shack was ticking like a clock.

Chapter Eleven

News of kidnapped passengers in a bus in Tarako province soon hit the airwaves when the kidnappers started making their ransom demands. When Petutu's wife heard the news, she hoped the passengers kidnapped were not those of the bus her husband was travelling in. When after two days of the announcement no one called her to make a ransom demand, her fear abated. But he had not called her and this was not like him. He always called her even when he had not travelled but was not at home. Not only had he not called her, she had called him several times, but the answering machine kept saying his number was not available. Fear for his safety mounted in her. She mourned her fear to Hacham her friend.

Hacham was a woman who was not good in consoling people. Instead of consoling someone in grief, she often compounded the grief by saying the wrong thing. When Petutu's wife expressed her fear to her, instead of her allaying her friend's fear, she said, let it be only the number that is not available. Let him be available. If he is available, the number will be available one day.'

'What was that?' Petutu's wife flared up. 'You wish my husband dead? I should have known better not to express my anxiety to you.'

'I did not mean it that way,' Hacham said. 'But you know how dangerous this country has become. When someone leaves home, you can only be sure he is alive and well when he returns.'

'My husband is alive and well,' Petutu's wife said, sniffing.

'Let's hope so,' her friend said.

'Please, leave my house,' Petutu's wife said leaving the frontage of the house she and her friend were to re-enter the house. Soon she was out of the house again heading out of the village. Her friend having failed to console her, she was going to Etete jungle to seek consolation. In superstition and love of nature, she was very much like her husband. Twice she had been to Etete jungle with her husband and seemed to like it as much as he did. If she did not enter it as frequently as he did, it was because he was a man and she was a woman. Women entered a forest either to fetch firewood or water. It was odd seeing a woman coming out of a forest without a pot of water or a bundle of firewood on her head. Men entered a forest to hunt, set traps for animals and honey bees and for the fun of it. So, it was quite normal seeing a man coming out of a forest without anything on his head or in his hands.

In Etete jungle, she went to sit by Ahok stream. Though a woman, her friends kept telling her she had the heart of a man. They said so because she went to places women feared to go. No woman would want to enter Etete jungle and sit by Ahok stream the way she was now doing.

Ahok stream was the last place her husband visited before he left for Tarako. He told her he went to the stream to commune with nature and his ancestors for the safety and success of his trip. She was also by the stream to commune with nature and his ancestors for the safety of the trip if not its success. She never wanted him to embark on the trip in the first place. But since he insisted and had his way, she was by the stream to supplicate with nature and the ancestors to keep him safe.

To Petutu's wife, trees and shrubs by the banks of Ahok stream looked greener and lusher than trees elsewhere. Breeze from the stream was fresher and more intimate than breeze from elsewhere. Sitting on the bank of the stream mumbling words of prayers, she could see ashen and shadowing human figures walking the banks of the stream and bending down to fetch its water. She was awe-struck. This was the third time she was seeing these images by the stream. She was as awe-struck now as she was the other times she saw them. One of the shadowy figures that walked past her looked like her husband. Fear replaced reverence in her heart. Had her husband died and joined his ancestors by Ahok stream? For a while, her heart stopped beating, then began beating violently.

'No, my husband is not dead; he is alive,' she said when she recovered her breath. 'He could not have commune with nature and his ancestors by this stream only for them to deliver him to death.'

As she sat by the stream, a dove cooed above her. She looked up and saw the dove. Like her husband and many people in Fakwa, the dove to her was a message bearer.

'Dove what news do you bring from my husband or from his ancestors?' she beseeched the dove earnestly.

The dove cooed several more times, skidded about in the air before perching on a tall tree a little far off the stream.

Petutu's wife stood up and began walking back home in deep thoughts. Seeing her face, it was difficult knowing if she was happier now than

she was when she went to the forest for succour or
she was sadder.

Chapter Twelve

For three days, Petutu and fellow hostages remained holed-up in the kidnappers' shack fed mainly with rice and soft drinks. For obvious reasons, the kidnappers were particularly more mean and cruel to Petutu than to other hostages. It was clear to him they were only keeping him alive either to get a ransom paid on him or prolong his suffering and not because they had any intention of allowing him walk away from them alive. Their leader had said that much.

Four days on with no ransom paid on any of the hostages, fear and desperation began to creep into the kidnappers' minds. With fear and desperation came spite and vindictiveness towards the hostages. There was the alarming and embarrassing case of the little boy hostage that Petutu and his fellow hostages met when they were brought to the kidnappers' hideout. The boy was apparently from a very poor home. When they made him call his father, the father laughed when they demanded one million dilas ransom on him. The father's laughter was like a knife driven through the heart of the leader of the kidnappers who made the demand. The father of the boy laughing this hauntingly either meant he did not care for his son or he had no money near what they were demanding. What followed soon told him which was the case. When the leader of the kidnappers handed the phone back to the little boy to try to speak sense into his father, the conversation between the little boy and his father settled the boy's case as a bad one.

'Papa!' the boy shouted excitedly to his father. 'They are feeding me with rice and coke here.'

'Is that so my son?' the father asked, excitedly.

'Yes papa,' the little boy said without a drop in his excitement.

'Then tell them to come kidnap the rest of the family,' the father said in a voice that carried a whip for the kidnappers.

The leader of the kidnappers snatched the phone from the boy to end his torment.

Petutu and other hostages listened to the little boy's conversation with his father with brightening faces if the kidnappers listened with darkening faces. It was to most of the hostages a comic relief in a tragic situation. When the leader of the kidnappers snatched the phone from the little boy to end his anguish, Petutu almost burst out laughing. The conversation of the little boy with his father reminded him of a chain-smoking professor who armed robbers invaded his house. Unruffled, the professor told the armed robbers they did not do their homework well before coming to his house for money. If they had, they would have gotten intelligence he had no money. The only thing he had was cigarettes. If they wanted to smoke, here were cigarettes. Hissing, the armed robbers left the house of the professor in anger.

Four days on and no ransom paid on any of the hostages, the kidnappers were visibly angry and agitated. Sitting alone and thinking, the leader of the kidnappers was full of questions with few answers. What was going on? Has the little boy and his parents infected relations of other hostages with their nonchalant attitude? Was it a case of them kidnapping poor people who could not pay their ransoms or were their ransoms too high for relations of their captives? Sue a pauper, reap a louse; was that the case here? Were they themselves hostages of greed? If they were, it seemed they were no less fearful than their captives. They had heard cases of kidnappers demanding ransoms of small amounts of money or even bags of rice. But kidnaping is a serious business with grave consequences that should not be so trivialized. No, they were not yet so cheap to be kidnapping people for pittance.

Should they have just robbed the passengers in the broken bus instead of embarking on the expensive enterprise of abducting them? But they were not pickpockets out for nickels and dimes. They were highwaymen out for high stakes. Still, was it a smart thing to have kidnapped the passengers of the bus who were turning out to be bad market? So far, no ransom had dropped on the head of any of the hostages and they were saddled with the expense of feeding them until ransoms were paid on them. The money they collected from the captives was fast getting spent on buying food for them and there was yet nothing to show for all their trouble. They had been left holding the short end of the stick which they were swinging about without hitting anyone. Their leader called a meeting of four of them behind the shack but not within earshot of the hostages. 'I am getting worried the way things are going,' he said where they were meeting.

'Worried is an understatement,' said one of the other three kidnappers with the leader. 'I am alarmed. If we are not careful, we will get nothing from relations of these hostages. This is bad market.'

'It is indeed bad market,' said the second kidnapper.

'What then do we do?' the leader asked probing their faces.

'I suggest we lower our ransom demands,' said the first kidnapper. 'Things are very hard in the country. We have all heard of kidnappers kidnapping people for bags of rice or even tiers of beans.'

'What do you think?' the leader asked the other two kidnappers

'I think the same way,' the second kidnapper said.

'I also think the same way,' said the third kidnapper.

'In the meantime, they can starve to death,' the leader said full of spite and anger. 'Perhaps it is because we are feeding them that is why their relations do not bother to pay the ransoms.'

'You are right boss,' said the third kidnapper. 'Imagine what that little boy was saying to his father and what the father was saying to him. We have been feeding them as if they were prisoners in a Swedish prison.'

'That is all over now,' the leader swore. 'No ransom money, but ransom feeding; no way.'

The four kidnappers all walked back to the shack to implement their decisions.

Chapter Thirteen

In Ase, mourners kept trooping into Ekete's house. Ekete was a good man. The multitude of mourners who trooped to his house on his death testified to his goodness. The house was swarming with people as a beehive with bees. People sitting; people standing; people pacing about; all talking in hushed tones about the goodness of the dead man.

Pleased as Ekete's wife was with the mammoth crowd her husband's death attracted, the burden of feeding the crowd of mourners was proving too heavy for her. For seven days during the wake-keeping, food was cooked in a big drum to feed people coming to condole with the family. Good in life, it was like people expected Ekete to continue to be good in death by feeding them. While some people went back to their houses to eat and return later, majority of the people remained in the house throughout the day only returning home at night to sleep.

Cooking food to feed people during funerals in Ase was relatively of recent origin. In the olden days, no one went to a funeral with expectations of eating food in the bereaved house. The event was too sombre for that. However, recently, funerals had turned into carnivals of feasting no less than wedding ceremonies. When funerals were not attended by feasting, they were burials simpliciter. There was no talk of ceremony. But when feasting was added to the solemn event, funerals became funeral ceremonies with all the pomp and pageantry that went with marriage or chieftancy ceremonies.

Not wanting to miss out on the wining and dining that now went with funeral ceremonies, elders of Ase evolved a taboo that forbade two people being buried in the town the same weekend. This taboo was more stringent and unrelenting if the dead person was old. There was always more food and drinks in burial ceremonies of old people. The children of the dead man or woman, if doing well financially, always wanted to make a statement during the burial ceremony of any of their parents. Since they might not be able to attend two or more funeral ceremonies to partake in the feasting there, elders of the town decreed that it was a taboo to bury two people – especially old people, on one weekend. With this taboo in force, they were sure of not missing out on any feasting in a funeral ceremony because they were attending another. With this taboo in force, they were sure of a feast almost every weekend because funeral ceremonies were now spread out over virtually all weekends. The elders of the town had so entrenched the taboo that relations of dead people now went to them to seek convenient dates to bury their dead the way lawyers seek convenient dates from judges to adjourn their cases to. Sometimes to get a convenient date, relations of a dead person may have to part with something to the elders.

'It is not only the living that attend funeral ceremonies; the ancestors also attend these ceremonies,' the elders kept saying. How were the ancestors to attend all funeral ceremonies if two or more of such ceremonies took place in one weekend? If the ancestors could not attend a funeral ceremony, it meant the dead person whose ceremony they could not attend would not be received in the land of the dead. He may even be banished from the land of the dead and would return to the land of the living to haunt his relations who caused his banishment. On the other hand, dead people whose funeral ceremonies the ancestors attended were not only admitted to the land of the dead by the ancestors, they were well attended to.

If the ancestors attended funeral ceremonies like the living as the elders claimed, the ancestors did not seem to be given much food and drinks in these ceremonies like the living. Only miserly liquor was poured on the ground for them to drink and only miserly food was thrown on the ground for them to eat.

Mourners in Ekete's house were so many that they spilled out of the courtyard to the neighbourhood of the house. Two men sitting outside the house were conversing animatedly between themselves.

'If there are weddings made in heaven, there are also funeral ceremonies made in heaven,' one of the two men said to the other.

'You are right,' said the other man. 'Since I could not choose how I was born, I should be able to choose how I will be buried. This is how I will like to be buried.'

'I have the same aspirations as you on this,' said the first man. 'This kind of burial would surely clothe one in the hereafter where one had been naked on earth, and feed one in the hereafter where one had been hungry on earth.'

'The sad thing is that turning round does not place one's buttocks in front of one,' said the second man.

'What does that mean?' the first man asked, sharply.

'You know what it means,' said the second man.

'Yeah, what is impossible cannot be made possible by wishes,' the first man said in a drawl. 'It is nigh impossible for either of us to have a funeral near this.'

'You can now see things the way I am seeing them,' said the second man. 'The condition one meets in a river determines the kind of fish he will catch. The conditions in my river and yours will not allow for this type of funeral.'

Chapter Fourteen

The leader of the kidnappers and his men were shocked to find Tobby their colleague they left in the shack to guard the hostages lying unconscious on the ground with all the hostages gone. For sometimes the four kidnappers stood looking at the scene in utter disbelief. It was like they were dreaming. What they were seeing could not be true in real life. Twice, the leader of the gang shook his head and pinched himself to wake up, but the nightmare persisted.

When it became clear to the kidnappers they were staring at stark reality, shame and fear for a while immobilized them. Numbed by common shame and fear into inaction, they were by a common mind of anger mobilized into action. The leader of the gang kicked the unconscious body of Tobby cursing and swearing at him in anger and contempt. What an apology of a goat! Left alone with yam, he could not eat the yam; the yam ate him. It was clear to him what happened. The hostages were not rescued by law enforcement officers. They rescued themselves. If law enforcement officers had rescued them, they wouldn't have left their colleague lying on the ground; they would have carried him with them.

They wouldn't even had left; they would have waited for them to show up. He shouldn't have forgotten so fast how one of the hostages had attacked them in a bid to abort his kidnap. If the hostages rescued themselves, he was very sure that fellow played a major role in them achieving this feat. But how could the hostages have rescued themselves chained as they were? Could someone other than themselves or law enforcement agents have rescued them? This seemed more probable. Who could that someone be? A hunter, a passer-by or someone the hostages called to rescue them? But how could they have called such a person when they had seized all their phones? How could anyone overcome his man and rescue the hostages without him or his other three men hearing or seeing what was happening? How could the hostages have freed themselves from their chains without him or any of his men being alerted by some sound or movement? Though they were out of earshot of the shack, they were not that far off not to be alerted by a rescue of this magnitude.

While their leader was kicking the body of Tobby, the other kidnappers ran out of the shack searching for the direction the hostages escaped through. They whirled round looking for where grasses or shrubs were bending, but saw nothing of the sort.

The leader of the gang soon came out of the shack and joined his men outside. 'What has happened is very serious,' he said to them. 'Though I am angry with Tobby for allowing it happened, I am also angry with myself, with three of you for allowing it happened. If Tobby is an apology of a goat, we are all apologies of goats.'

At this point, a movement behind him made the leader of the kidnappers swung round. It was Tobby. He had come to in the shack and was joining his comrades.

'Tobby, how could you; how could you allow this happen to us?' the leader of the gang wailed, shaking Tobby violently.

'Honestly boss, I don't know who or what hit me from behind,' Tobby mourned. 'It was too noiseless, too fast and too violent for me to respond.'

'We must go after them and bring them back,' the leader said. 'They couldn't have gone far. If we allow them escape, we are sunk. If we allow them escape, we need not come back here because the police and the army would be waiting for us.' Saying this, he parcelled the gang into three search groups and bade them run into the forest and fished out the hostages.

Chapter Fifteen

The leader of the kidnappers was right in his thinking that the hostages did not rescue themselves nor were they rescued by law enforcement agents, but by a third party. A man travelling to Tarako in his old ford seized by dysentery had stopped his vehicle near where the bus Petutu was travelling in was abandoned. The man rushed into the bush to relieve his bowels before he messes up his clothes and car. He was returning to his car by the roadside after relieving himself in the bush when he saw Petutu's phone lying under a little shrub. Believing the handset belonged to one of the passengers of the abandoned bus, he had picked it and hurried to his vehicle. The region he was he knew to be a dangerous region full of armed robbers and kidnappers. When dysentery had seized him in the region, he had cursed his luck, but had no choice but to stop.

When he had driven to a small village by the roadside, he stopped and tried switching on the phone he had found. But it did not switch on. It seemed its battery was down. He plucked it to his car charger and it began charging. He was right

After the phone had charged a little, he switched it on and scrolled through its contacts. Among the names on the phone was ICE which he had on his own phone. ICE to him meant *In Case of Emergency*. He dialled the number with this acronym and a woman answered. It was Petutu's wife. Her voice was shrill with anxiety and excitement. 'My husband, my husband,' she shrieked into the phone.

'It is not your husband,' the man who found the phone said.

'Who are you and what are you doing with my husband's phone?' the wife asked, her anxiety and fear rising to a feverish point.

'My name is Jodo. I found your husband's phone by the roadside near a vehicle he must have been travelling in which seemed to have been abandoned by the roadside,' Jodo said.

'You only saw the phone, but did not see my husband?' the wife wailed.

'No, I did not see your husband; neither did I see anyone by the abandoned vehicle,' Jodo said.

'My ancestors!' the woman exclaimed in terror. The bus Jodo was talking about must be the bus whose passengers were kidnapped. Her husband had been kidnapped. 'I told him not to embark on this journey, but he would not listen;

now look at what his stubbornness has brought upon us.'

'It is either your husband and other passengers in the bus boarded other vehicles and proceeded to their various destinations if their vehicle had broken down or they were the bus passengers that were kidnapped,' Jodo said.

'That's my fear,' Petutu's wife said, beside herself with fear.

'These days, there are news of kidnapping all over the country,' Jodo said. 'Where their vehicle was abandoned is full of kidnappers. I won't be surprised if they were kidnapped.'

'My ancestors!' Petutu's wife exclaimed again in agony. 'I also think they were kidnapped. But if they were, why have the kidnappers not contacted me for a ransom?'

'Perhaps because they don't have your telephone number,' Jodo said. 'Remember your husband is not with his phone. Unless he has your number by heart, neither he nor his captors can call you.'

'You are right,' the woman said. 'My ancestors, I am finished.'

'Where was your husband travelling to?' Jodo asked.

'Tarako,' Petutu's wife said.

'What was he going to Tarako to do?' Jodo asked a random question he did not know why he asked.

'He said he was going to deliver messages Ekete his friend who died in the Pokko war asked him to deliver to his wife,' Petutu's wife said.

'My ancestors!' the man exclaimed. 'I hope this Ekete you are talking about is not my sister's husband that died a few weeks ago in the Pokko war?' the man said more to himself than to Petutu's wife.

'What!' Petutu's wife exclaimed in shock. 'He is most likely to be the one. My husband only returned from the war a few weeks back.'

'My ancestors,' Jodo said, drawing a long breath. 'How was I to know, a phone I found in the bush belonged to a man taking messages to my sister?'

'My husband,' Petutu's wife mourned.

'Don't worry,' Jodo said. 'Ekete's wife is my only sister. Whoever is taking messages to her from her late husband is a friend. I know very well the area your husband's journey was truncated. Give me a few days. I will surely turn up something.'

Chapter Sixteen

Jodo truly knew not only the area he found Petutu's phone as he said to Petutu's wife, but most of Tarako province. He was born in Tarako and had all his life lived and worked in different parts of the province. He was an outgoing man with a lot of social contacts. In addition, he was an immensely capable man when it came to investigating and tracking crime. His friends had told him he would have done better as a police officer than the railway worker he was. They said he was the hare in the jungle who knew how to track down the wily chameleon.

'Wherever the chameleon is in the forest ...' Tonga his friend used to say to him.

'The hare knows,' he would complete for him.

'If no one saw the tortoise in the barn of the rabbit ...'

'The hare saw him.'

'If no one sees the drummer beating the drums for the antelope to dance ...'

'The hare sees him.'

Buoyed by confidence in his ability to investigate and burst crimes, Jodo rarely relied on the police to investigate crimes that affected him.

He investigated them himself using his enormous social contacts. In the course of time, he had developed disdain for the police. Their incompetence bred by corruption always riled him. He saw himself as his own best policeman.

When he finished talking with Petutu's wife, he reached out to people he knew in the district of the province for intelligence on possible kidnappers' hideouts in the region. It did not take him long to find out possible locations the kidnapped passengers were likely to be held hostages. He sneaked to three of such possible locations, but found nothing. It was the fourth location he visited that turned out to be where Petutu and other passengers of the bus were held hostages.

Jodo did not know for sure the shack he saw in the middle of the forest was where Petutu and other hostages were holed in. But he knew it must be a criminal hideout from its looks and location. He was soon proved right when two of the kidnappers came out of the shack guns in hands.

For hours, Jodo lurked about the forest the hostages were held, waiting for an opportunity he would walk to the shack and see what was inside it. Keenly observing the kidnappers as they came out and went into the shack, he determined they were either four or slightly above this number. He would wait until some necessity took all or a substantial number of them away from the shack, then he would move in to try rescuing inmates in the shack if there were such inmates.

The opportunity Jodo was looking for came when the leader of the kidnappers and three of his men left the shack to meet somewhere behind the shack. Moving like a shadow, he closed in on the shack. From where he was lurking in front of the shack, he could see the remaining kidnapper sitting on a tree stump outside the shack with his gun on his laps. His head kept lurching forward only for him to snap it back. He was sleeping. Moving swiftly but noiselessly, Jodo hit him hard on the back of his head with the butt of his gun. He fell down on his face with only a tiny groan of pain.

When Jodo appeared in front of the shack gun in hand, the hostages instinctively felt he was there to rescue them. They were all joy. When he hit the kidnapper with the butt of his gun, their instinctive feelings were confirmed.

Seeing the hostages in chains secured to pegs, Jodo for a while was dismayed.

'The keys to our chains are in his pocket,' Petutu said observing Jodo's dismay.

Quickly, Jodo searched the pockets of the unconscious kidnapper, found the keys and snapped off the chains on the hostages. Together, they fled the shack.

The kidnappers searched the forest for the hostages but did not find them. While they were searching for the hostages, Jodo had crammed them into a bus he brought with him and was driving them to Tarako town.

Chapter Seventeen

Jodo carried the freed hostages straight to the police station in Tarako. This was about the fourth time he was delivering to the police trophies they ought to have won. They were not finding this funny and had always told him so. His action exposed them at an embarrassing point. Why did he find it so difficult working with them when he had a tip-off on a crime? Working with him, they will give him covering fire.

But Jodo would not bite the police offer. He liked working alone. He was an adventurous man who liked flirting with danger not out of a quest for heroism, but out of the thrill of flirting with risk. Again, he neither trusted the police nor credit them with competence to give him covering fire. So, he continued to work alone on his crime-bursting hobby.

While driving the hostages to the police station, Jodo had asked them whether there was one among them called Petutu.

'I am Petutu,' Petutu said eagerly, wondering how Jodo came by his name.

'Petutu, where were you travelling to when you were kidnapped?' Jodo asked, peremptorily.

'I was going to Tarako,' Petutu said wondering why his destination should be of interest to Jodo.

'What were you going to Tarako to do?' Jodo asked again in the same imperial tone.

'I was going to deliver messages a fellow combatant killed in the Pokko war asked me to deliver to his widow,' Petutu said, feeling uneasy.

Jodo did not say anything again as he drove the rescued hostages towards Tarako. At the police station, he drew Petutu aside and told him he was the brother of the widow he was going to Tarako to deliver messages to.

'Incredible!' Petutu muttered.

'Yet very true,' Jodo said.

'How do you know me and what was taking me to Tarako?' Petutu asked without let in his amazement.

'On our way here, you told me your name and what was taking you to Tarako,' Jodo said.

'That's true,' Petutu said, laughing. What Jodo just said reminded him of an incidence between the Fobo and Bambam tribe. The two tribes lived in one community. At some point, there was an increase in the incidence of crime in the community. It was discovered that most of the crimes were committed by young men of the community. Thereupon, elders from the two tribes that made up the community met to deliberate on how to tackle the menace. At the end of their meeting, the elders decided it would be the responsibility of the elders of a tribe to report to the council of elders any crime committed by a young man of the tribe. For a while this arrangement worked well. Later however, elders of the Bambam tribe felt that elders of the Fobo tribe had not been reporting their young men who committed crime the way they had been reporting their own young men. When a young man of Bambam that committed a crime was reported to the council of elders and an elder of the Fobo tribe nicknamed *local barrister* descended heavily on the young man with verbal insults, an elder from the Bambam tribe told him to take it easy, after all, elders of the Fobo tribe had not been as forthcoming as his own tribe in reporting their delinquent youths.

The Fobo elder seeming to be taken aback by this charge asked the Bambam elder to prove his allegation. Thereupon the Bambam elder asked the Fobo elder if he can swear he had not heard that Choja a young man of the Fobo tribe stole someone's chicken recently.

'How can I swear I have not heard when you just told me?' the Fobo tribe elder said, a faint smile perched on his lips.

Everyone laughed, some punctuating their laughter with salutations of 'local barrister.'

'Seriously, how do you know me?' Petutu asked Jodo when the two men stopped laughing.

'Through your phone,' Jodo said bringing out Petutu's phone from his pocket.

For a while, Petutu with a look of shock stared at the phone in Jodo's hand without saying anything. 'Where did you find it?' he finally asked when he overcame his shock.

'Where you were kidnapped,' Jodo said.

'Life!'Petutu exclaimed in amazement. 'How then do you know it is my phone? My name is not written on it.'

'I called the number bearing ICE in your phone and your wife answered my call.'

'Life!' Petutu exclaimed again. 'When I lost my phone where our vehicle broke down, I was sad I could not call my wife to tell her our vehicle had broken down on the road. How was I to know the phone got lost to fall into the hands of the man that will rescue me from kidnappers and lead me to the widow I set out in search of?'

'That's how life can be sometimes,' Jodo said. 'What you think is good may turn out bad and what you think is bad may turn out good. There is often no telling what the outcome of a thing will be.'

Chapter Eighteen

'Ebelebe!' Petutu drawled when the doves had completely disappeared in the distant horizon. The doves had brought him outside his house where he and Oliki his neighbour stood looking at the doves and listening to their cooing. When the doves disappeared in the horizon, the two men sat on a cement embankment attached to the fence of the house. It was one of those cool days Petutu loved sitting in front of his house to absorb the passing breeze. He had always thought that the breeze blowing through his house was more than the breeze blowing through other houses. He often said breeze was planted somewhere near his house and he would seek out where it was planted and irrigate it.

To Petutu, a cold early morning breeze did not only breed health, it bred youth. He was a deeply superstitious man who believed that if a person washes his face with dew and breathe in the early morning breeze, the person will be as youthful as the morning. It was a belief he did not know how he came by. That he did not know how he came by the belief did not in any way temper its rigor in him. Since his youth, he had always gone into the bush in the morning whenever there was dewfall to wash his face with dew. If the dew was much and no one was about, he removed his clothes and rubbed the dew on all parts of his body his hands could reach. One day he was in the bush washing his face with dew when he saw a tortoise crawling by. For a while, he stopped what he was doing to regard the tortoise. From the way the tortoise was moving, it seemed it neither saw nor sensed his presence. He stood still not making any movement to keep affairs between him and the tortoise the way they were. He not only loved the tortoise, he respected it. Its intelligence and exploits in the folklore of the clan recommended it for respect. The longevity of the tortoise was another reason he respected it. He had heard that the tortoise can live as long as three hundred years. He attributed the tortoise's longevity to its survival skills and unemotional attitude to life. Looking at the tortoise crawling towards him now, he wondered how old it was. With a thick shell over it, it must be difficult even for animals to tell the age of a tortoise. If it had wrinkles, the shell would cover them. If it was greying, so long as the greying was not on its shell, no animal would see the greying. Unlike him, the tortoise may not even need the dew he was washing his face with to stay young. Ironically, it was the tortoise that did not need dew for youthfulness that dew was always falling on. Life is fond of passing favours over those who need them to those who don't.

At this point, the tortoise if it had not seen him had sensed his presence. It was no longer moving. It stood in one place, its head occasionally turning from side to side perhaps collecting more intelligence on his presence.

Thinking the tortoise must have either seen him or sensed his presence and he had nothing more to gain by standing still, he spoke to the tortoise, 'Old and crafty one of the forest,' he saluted the tortoise.

The tortoise hearing his voice changed direction and crawled away from him. The speed with which it crawled away was amazing to him. It was like it did not crawl but slithered away like a snake. 'No wonder,' he muttered. 'No wonder.'

This was many years ago. Now Petutu above middle-age, looked much younger than his age. He attributed his youthfulness to washing his face with dew and rubbing what he called the elixir of youth round his body. Now sitting with Oliki in front of his house, he seemed full of cheer and youthfulness. 'Ebelebe,' he intoned with gusto and a certain measure of charm that contrasted sharply with Oliki's rather drawn face.

Oliki did not say anything. He seemed lost in thoughts.

'I can't understand why men are fighting over land that would eventually swallow them?' Petutu wondered aloud.

'They are only fighting over land and water now,' Oliki said, pertly. 'The way things are going in the land of men, tomorrow they will fight over the sky.'

'Tienko is sick,' Petutu said. 'Why go to war over a Penisula we all know is not ours?'

'Because there is oil in it,' Oliki said. 'If it were a peninsula of sand, no one will fight over it.'

'Tienko is sick and should be taken to the hospital,' Petutu repeated more to himself t.han to Oliki.

'As for being sick, it is not only Tienko that is sick; the whole world is sick,' Oliki said.

Petutu did not say anything. It was clear he was in deep thoughts; but it was not so clear what he was thinking about.

From where the two men were sitting, they could see two hawks circling the sky a little far off. Soon the two hawks were joined by other hawks and doves all circling the sky to the astonishment of the two men and other people in the village. The birds in the sky were so many that they formed a cloud that blocked the sun. For quite some time, they circled the sky screeching and cooing in a rowdy way that suggested a party. When people were beginning to wonder how long they would remain in the sky, they filed away and disappeared in the distant horizon.

'Ebelebe!' Petutu exclaimed.

'Ebelebe,' Oliki enthused.

'What is happening in the sky?'

'What is happening on earth should be the question?' Oliki said. 'The sky is merely expressing what is happening on earth.'

'What is happening on earth that the sky is expressing?' Petutu asked, looking at Oliki with rising excitement.

'War; war is happening everywhere in the world; war has overtaken the earth,' Oliki said in a dramatic tone. 'This is what the sky is expressing. A cold war of cultural conflict between the west and the east is now warming into a hot war of economic interest that will leave millions of people dead.'

'Ebebele,' Petutu yelled.

'Ebebele,' Oliki enthused.

'Which do you choose?' Petutu asked.

'I choose peace of course!' Oliki said.

'A choice of gold,' Petutu cooed.

'You and I may choose peace, but does our choice matter that much in a world that seems to have chosen war?' Oliki asked his whole being overtaken by a sombre mood. 'Does our choice really matter?'

'Oliki!' Petutu bellowed.